MW00332252

WAX

Wax

Padraig Hogan

QUERENCIA

Querencia Press, LLC
Chicago, Illinois

ISBN
978 1 959118 34 3

www.querenciapress.com

First Published in 2023

Querencia Press, LLC
Chicago IL

Printed & Bound in the United States of America

To Lelly, from Patch
Without you I would never have written a coherent word.

CONTENTS

BLAME

It wasn't his fault.

Not really.

But by the way he alternated between chewing on his nails and digging at his cuticles when he gave his report to the police, it was clear there was no convincing him of that. As for the other kids, well, they bolted at the first sign of trouble, what with them all being at least seven years younger than him. He could have been tried as an adult—the last thing they wanted was to be considered an accessory. Not that he couldn't have kept them there. With his husky figure and deep voice, just one insistent *wait* was all it would have taken to stop them cold. And later when he told their parents it wasn't his fault, well, even though he didn't really believe it, it really wasn't.

Probably.

That is to say, he did go into the basement where his little brother was playing with his friends. And sure, he was the one who invited them to go, coaxing them with promises of adventure and local legends and threats of being called chicken. And it wouldn't be a falsehood to say some of his intentions teetered away from the purely good. And trying to explain where he got the fireworks would prove troublesome. But it was their own dumb fault for going with him, right? After all, if two heads are better than one, then five must be a collage of good decision-making and all five of their heads agreed with his one head, so they should be five times at fault.

Five times, at *least.*

After all, the five of them had seen the warning signs just as well as he had. Literal signs, more signs than visible fence, warning against trespassing. Guarantees of impending doom.

But the group could only focus on the small gap between those warnings, a slight absence of fence that had been cut and mended and recut so many times there were mismatched and misshapen bits of metal combined with twist ties and planks of wood strewn everywhere.

And it could maybe be argued that he shouldn't have held open the fence to let in the five boys. But then, pretending to close it on his little brother when it was his turn to pass, could be seen as a bonding moment. Who can argue against brotherly bonding? This whole adventure was about tradition, after all. And what's more important than tradition?

He could tell the boys were tense. In a small town like theirs, everyone knew about that fence. It was practically a rite of passage to explore back there. Schoolyards spread rumors of the unspeakable horrors the fence contained. Some children would sneak there at night and claim the next morning they had seen the ghosts of all the kids who had died beyond the fence, claim they could still hear their moans and screams. Based on the old blankets and used condoms that came into view once they got their bearings on the other side, the part about the noises probably wasn't a lie. Sometimes people probably went there to get drunk and use their empty cans and bottles for target practice, leaving broken glass and crumpled aluminum everywhere. The truth is, there wasn't much to see on that half acre. A lot full of overgrowth and litter, mostly. And from where he stood, the sun illuminated the whole thing. The plot was on a downward slant and the broken section of fence was at the top.

The boys hadn't moved since they went through. They instead huddled together, not looking beyond what was directly in front of them for fear of what they would see. At their age, it was normal to stop being afraid of the fence, almost like losing a belief in Santa. But no one fully loses that fear until after their first time on the other side.

Now, here, it could probably be argued that it *was* his fault.

Probably.

Because, see, he knew they'd be spooked. He had been spooked his first time, too. Everyone is. So, when he stood on his toes and craned his neck and gasped, the kids jumped a bit. And when, after making sure he was positioned right in front of the part of the fence they could escape through, he breathed, "They're awake."

They stood on their toes and craned their necks too, but they thought him being taller meant he could see something they couldn't. So, when, as a group, they backed toward the fence without breaking their collective gaze from the threatening unknown, he pulled out his lighter, found the fuse, and tossed the small pack of firecrackers behind him.

Two of the kids went in opposite directions, running along the fence; one of them dropped and cowered on the spot, and the final two, one of whom was his brother, bolted through the weeds. After a beat and through laughter, he tried to tell the cowering kid that it was all a joke, that he would be fine, that they should go look for the others, but before he had the chance he heard a scream from out in the field.

A real one.

He knew what had happened before he saw it. See, there's a reason that area is blocked off, a reason beyond childhood superstition. The lot was deemed unsafe by the county because it was hollow underneath. About a hundred feet from the fence was an old mine shaft hosting an almost vertical drop about ten yards down. It had been haphazardly covered with some plywood that had since been hidden by a thin layer of dirt and weeds. But it was intended to prevent animals from falling in and potentially contaminating the groundwater, not to support the weight of a scared boy.

He made it to the mouth of the mineshaft and saw one of his brother's friends standing over the hole, recently displaced dust still hanging in the air. He approached slowly, lightly pushing the kid away as he peered in. The scream had been loud enough to regain the focus of the rest of the kids and the other three joined them. The sun was angled in such a way that it was too dark to see in the hole.

He called his brother's name.

He called it again.

He cursed under his breath.

A scream echoed from the bottom of the mine and hung in the air like smoke, thick and wet and shrill against their ears.

Silence.

And this is when the four kids ran.

And this next part was most definitely his fault, even if the county should have maintained the lot better to prevent just this sort of thing.

See, the boys ran back toward the cut in the fence, but they were greeted by a growing fire. The sparks from the firecrackers were more than enough for the dry plant life. They turned to run toward the bottom of the field, almost falling down the shaft to join their friend before realizing where they were and skirting around it, giving the two brothers a wide berth. He could hear them helping each other scale the ten-foot fence at the bottom, a yelp of pain where one of them caught on the barbed wire, a cry of fear when the last one inside realized their mistake clambering the chain link, the fading clap of sneakers on pavement as they sprinted away.

But he stayed. He couldn't leave his brother down there. He tried to stay as near the edge of the mine as he could to keep away from the fire. After all, he had the advantage of being downhill, but the fire was having no trouble engulfing the dry weeds.

It didn't take long before he had to decide between running from the fire or joining his little brother, and it would definitely be his fault if he abandoned his brother. So, he pressed himself as flat as he could against the exposed wall of the mine shaft and did his best to slide down with only his shoes to slow him.

The air down there was stale. The suddenness of it combined with the heat of the fire and the smoke bearing down on him and the trapped dust made him cough. It didn't take long for him to find his brother, cold and still and unmoving.

The police said after they put out the fire, which at that point had left a clear path through much of the weeds, he wasn't crying.

Actually, they said he hadn't cried.

With that much dirt caked on the sweat on his face, it was impossible to hide whether or not he'd been crying. The only time he reacted wasn't when they pulled out his brother, but when he watched two other officers cross under the police tape and toss a piece of plywood over the open mouth of the mine before tying together the broken part of the fence with some loose wire.

Afterward, when no charges were filed because his father threatened to sue the county for negligence and when his mother could look him in the eye again and when he could finally get out of bed, he went back.

Just to see.

The ties were cut, and the new boards were set aside.

Somewhere in the air he could hear moans and screams.

ANIMAL

But the animal itself, the father never would have let the child play with it. Its fur, matted and dirty, seeped the rain from the previous night when she squeezed it. It had rained the year before too, he remembered. Everyone remembered.

And the car had long been pulled from the creek, but the saplings that grew along its edges were still bent in half, trying to survive with what water they could get when the creek was high enough. This time of year, it was always high enough.

But one year later and here were waterlogged candles and flowers, the blackened sky and intentionless winds pulling and threatening to interfere.

And this animal could have been one from last night or one from last year, the father wasn't sure, but regardless, it didn't belong to her—although who did it belong to? What was the timeline for when a roadside memorial becomes litter?

But she's not asking for permission anymore, holding it out to him. No, she's squeezing it against herself, her sweater soaking as the animal squelches, drips onto the sidewalk, a mildewed smell entering the air even in these low temperatures.

And he tries to take it from her, at first with a gentle hand, then with a firmer one, his hand growing cold and wet and tired as he tugs at the arm, just enough held back not to harm it, but she screams all the same and he has to pull harder and she screams louder and now people are looking. Should he just let her have it for now? Try to clean it or throw it away when they're home?

But no, she's already soaked to her flesh and her mittens will be just as damp and she'll start shivering soon and it's still another thirty-minute walk home, so he gives it one last good yank and it slides from her grip. Defeated, she cries, not trying to get it back but retreating into herself and the father walks back to the collection of artifacts and tries to find somewhere to place it but he's not sure where he can that doesn't feel like he's overtaking it or isolating it, and besides, he sees the child eyeballing it, waiting for him to put it down so she can snatch it up again.

And he looks to the creek and swears he can still see tire marks in the mud, but those had long been flattened, and the sound of the child is overtaken by the water as he tosses it in and doesn't even wait to hear the splash.

ATTIC

The first rain of the season is always the loudest. A barrage against the roof is an intrusive sound after six months of relative quiet. The sun attacks in secret; a storm announces its charge. So, it was no surprise when June woke in the middle of the night to the sound of distant thunder as it echoed over the expanse of trees and hills that surrounded her cabin.

It was the kind of sleep that doesn't depart right away. It floated just above her head, tendrils latched onto her scalp, dissipating into the void by indiscernible degrees, loosening its grip one spiral at a time. She did her best to fall back asleep. The sound of rain was supposed to soothe, after all. But as she lay there, she became more conscious of her body. The more she focused on the fact that she wasn't asleep, the more aware she became that sleep was eluding her.

As she took stock of herself, she realized her arm was hanging over the edge of the bed, leaving her hand bare before the gaping mouth that yawned beneath her sheets. She could just feel the threads of the carpet brushing her fingertips. She yanked back the hand and tucked it under her comforter for safety. A paranoia carried from childhood; her mother's voice echoing in her head telling her to keep her hands and feet inside the blankets at all times. Her whole left side tingled with the sudden shift in blood flow and she felt a tinge of jealousy that some part of her had managed to remain asleep. She extended her fingers, closed a fist, extended her fingers, closed a fist, until the feeling subsided.

As the prospect of sleep took its leave, boredom crept in. June was in a perpetual state of restlessness while she was awake, so when it came to sleep, she had to seize the opportunity the moment it presented itself, because when it was gone, it was gone. At this point, six months into staying in this cabin alone, she had a routine to get herself to sleep that usually worked and she hoped she could trick her mind into falling for it a second time in one night.

The first test of her will was to leave the warmth of her bed. Her robe was just across the room, hanging from a hook on the door with her slippers beneath. In the dark, they loomed, each corner and curve of the fabric creating a shadow on a shadow, threatening. She reached for the lamp on her bedside table, knocking over a thick book that had been resting there in the process. June stared at the book on the floor, the bookmark next to it, and sighed, defeated. She knew she would never find which page she had been on. Committing to the plunge, she inhaled through her nose and held her breath, uncovering herself and skittering toward warmth.

Even through her new layers, she still shivered when passing under the trapdoor to the attic. A string dangled just above her head, which once pulled, would expose a set of steps. The crisp air from the storm pushed through the room above creating a noticeable cold spot. She rushed through it.

The attic was where she did her work.

June first went into the kitchen and, after testing the weight and giving it a slosh to check the remaining water level, put on the kettle. As the water heated, she moved to the fireplace to add a few logs to the glowing embers that remained. She waited until they ignited before turning away.

From the window June could see the storm in all its glory. Beyond the cabin, the land dipped gradually before shooting up into expansive mountains high above her, giving her an almost unobstructed view of the trees, only blocked by other trees surrounding the cabin. Evergreens older than her, older than her grandparents probably, swayed and fought against the wind. The rain itself came in sideways and from all directions. Even the covered porch, which extended about ten feet from the front door, was soaked up to the cabin. She couldn't remember the last time she had seen a storm this size.

The sound of boiling water and crackle from the fireplace returned June's attention to the inside, and she turned off the burner as the kettle began to whistle, grabbing a mug from the cabinet and a teabag from the pantry. She breathed deeply through the teabag, enjoying its scent. Once it was steeped and sweetened, she took her place near the now roaring fire. She only had the one chair, placed perfectly for reading, not too close or far from the fireplace and not directly under any vents. The glow from the fire cast deep and tangled shadows against the wall to her right. She watched as her silhouette expanded and withdrew, a horrible twisting choreography against the blank canvas of the wall.

At first she thought her ears were playing tricks on her, that she could still hear the kettle whistling, until she realized it was the howl of the wind. The storm was getting stronger. From her chair she could see into the hallway; the string hung down from the ceiling. The air was still, but it seemed to move a little, a pendulum with no clear direction. She blew at the steam from her tea and took a testing sip before walking into the hallway and pulling down the steps to the attic above.

The stairs came down with a thud that still caught June off guard despite all the time she'd been there. This, coupled with the cold air that rushed to meet her, nearly made her drop her cup. Instead, some tea sloshed over the side, dampening her slippers and warming her feet. She sighed and rolled her eyes at herself, stepping heavily across the wooden boards and ascending into the darkness above.

It was a darkness she was not accustomed to.

Every morning June would wake with the sun and go to the attic to write. It was mostly empty except she'd had a large window put in overlooking the woods. The window faced east, so there was always more than enough sunlight in the morning, but the density of the woods prevented her from being blinded. June had never seen so many trees before moving there. They enclosed the house, an extra set of walls with no door. Along with the window she had bought a large, solid desk, which had to be moved in through the wall before the panes were installed.

She was there by suggestion of her publisher, though really, she saw no other option either. The diagnosis had been a bit of a shock, though not entirely. The doctors said it was genetic. They also said there was no preventing what was coming.

Flipping the switch on a rough, vertical beam gave life to a single exposed light bulb, flooding the room in a sickly yellow. June approached her desk, a sturdy piece of oak with a single drawer, a typewriter and a stack of papers. She placed her mug on the desk among dozens of brown rings from previous mornings' coffees and teas.

June ran her thumb along the corners of the papers, as if to count them, but she knew the total already. This was her finished novel. The reason she had come up here in the first place, to the quiet and seclusion of the woods. No distractions or outside responsibilities. The thrill she felt looking at the pages was short lived as June, remembering the time, or realizing it could be any time, cursed herself again for waking. This was supposed to be the first morning she'd allow herself to sleep in since moving here in the spring. The book was complete. She could rest her mind and sit in her chair and read what she had written. See what needed to be fixed. Instead, the rain had come.

Typically, she spent years on her novels. Her first had taken her almost a decade to complete, though back then she was working every day and was only writing for herself. She had never imagined it would turn into the beloved series it had. But when it did, the day she would write the final installation seemed a far-off dream. But now she had done it, and in only half a year. Time was of the essence. And she felt she owed it to everyone.

The wind outside shifted and a soft tapping began against the window. June retrieved her cup, holding it with both hands to try to keep warm, and approached the sound, watching the rain lash against the glass. The trees swayed and turned, shivering along with June, fighting to remain standing. A few branches that bordered the porch reached the panes, making their presence known. This was the only part of the house to which the trees didn't have direct access. In the distance a single bolt of lightning illuminated the sky before fading. Out of habit, June counted.

One.
Two.
Thr-

The thunder echoed through the house. Her eyes shifted focus and she saw her own reflection in the window. She knew she looked tired, but she also knew she had earned that tiredness.

She yawned. A good sign.

Another flash of lightning.

One.
Tw-

The trees continued their terrified sway as June moved to go back downstairs. The sudden change in temperature upon returning to the hallway sent a chill through her. She added another log to the fire and took a seat. Wind and rain pushed their way down the chimney, threatening to extinguish the remaining flame.

All sides of the house flashed white. June didn't make it to the count of one before the thunder hit. The entire house seemed to vibrate from the inside out. If the storm was overhead now, she hoped it would only get quieter from here on out. Allow her at least a few more hours of rest.

She gulped down the rest of her tea and rinsed the mug in the kitchen sink. There was no space now between the engulfing flashes and the windows rattling with such force she feared one may leak before it passed. The storm was the loudest it had been all night, as if she could hear each individual raindrop even as they hit simultaneously. After warming her hands against the now-dwindling fire, she slunk off toward her bedroom.

As she walked under the attic door, something cold dripped on her head. At first, she thought she'd imagined it, but when she ran her hand through her hair it came away wet. She examined her palm but couldn't make out any color in the dim light. There was no smell either. She reached toward the string that separated her from the attic, pinching her thumb and index finger along it, and sliding it down with some pressure. The entire thing was saturated and drip-drip-dripped onto the floor in front of her.

It took a few beats for her to recover from her newfound grogginess, but a horror shuddered through her body as she gripped the string and yanked. Narrowly dodging the steps as they banged onto the floor, she hurried upward.

She was soaked before she could take in the chaos surrounding her. First, she noticed the awful thickness that had overtaken her feet. By the time they reached level ground, her slippers were already sloshing and squelching. She absentmindedly removed them as she turned on the light and tried to decide where to look. Soaking in the water that now covered most of the floor, were sheets of paper, on some of which she realized she was standing. Her attention moved as she approached her desk. Even in the dim light she could see it was buckling under the weight of a large branch, which had forced its way through the window. Though her feet were numb, the realization that she was walking on shattered bits of glass made its way into her mind. More pressing, however, became the understanding that if she did not act quickly, her book would be lost forever.

June moved with a frantic focus, trying to peel the saturated sheets from the wooden floor without tearing them. There was no time to check their condition. She piled them together with as much neatness and speed as she could balance, pushing against the sharp rain as it blew at her, then away from her, then at her again with such force and irregularity, that she often lost her footing trying to match the storm's sway.

The bundle of soaking papers was growing in her arms; even against her already saturated body, she could feel the degree to which they had become sodden with water. She caught herself beginning to shake. Whether from cold or adrenaline, she couldn't be sure, but she knew she had to get back downstairs as soon as she could. Her frantic eyes searched for any remaining papers. As the wind shifted, it had enough strength to expose a paper here or there that was otherwise hiding in the shadows of the room. The single lightbulb did little to illuminate more than a few feet out, and June found herself more at the mercy of the lightning than anything else.

She climbed over the large branch that bisected the attic, hoping to see into all angles of the room, and not lose a single page. The wind came at her full force then, and as she shifted her weight a piece of broken window slid up into her foot. Even numb from cold, the pain shot through her and took her attention just long enough that some pages came loose and rejoined the rain. She snatched at them, exhausted. Additional pages left her grasp. She was quick to reclaim the ones on the floor, but the wind took three of the pages up toward the ceiling, fighting gravity and all of June's will, before sweeping them out of the window and onto the covered porch just below.

June was at a loss. Surely, she could rewrite three pages. Even if they weren't exact, they'd be close enough. After all, she wrote them before.

Unless she couldn't. Unless those were three irreplaceable pages. Unless the past six months had all been for nothing.

The wind pushed back through the window, pushed back against her. The pages caught on the wall just outside, just through the window. Maybe she could reach them. She knew she had to try.

The closer she got to the window, even without the wind shifting and directing itself at her, the more trouble she had keeping her footing. The only way she could keep her balance was to drag her feet forward, sliver of glass and all.

She was able to grab two of the pages with relative ease— relative ease considering—but the third was just out of reach, nearing the roof proper. She leaned out, but there was no way for her to grasp it, even standing on her toes. The wind pushed her back again, and out of instinct she reached out and grabbed the large pane, stabbing small shards of glass into her hands. A wave of frustration passed through her. Determined for the evening to end, she climbed on the branch still protruding from the window and braced herself against a beam above.

She leaned out into the storm.

In order to reach the last page, she would have to let go of the beam.

She focused on her center of gravity, found her balance and footing, and reached up blindly. It was too dark outside to see the faint detail of paper against the wall. Her hand was as numb as the rest of her, but she grasped at the air, trying to find anything that would come loose. A flash of lightning gave her just enough to bridge the gap between where she was grasping and where she needed to be. But as she snatched at the page, thunder ripped through the air.

She jumped slightly, relieving the pressure on her foot just enough that when she fully stood on it again, the pain from the glass was renewed. To regain her balance, she pushed her forearm against the wall, which put a thick shard of glass directly into it. This final assault was finished with a new gust of wind, which removed June from any stability she once had, dropping her to the attic floor.

The shock of the fall knocked the wind out of her. It took her a few moments before she realized that the papers were no longer in her arms. She looked through the opening, unfazed by what berated her, and saw her papers scattering about in the mud, catching on branches, floating in puddles.

Pure resolve sent her back toward the stairs. As she descended, her foot, irritated by the glass and soaked with blood and rain, lost its grip. She slid forward, landing on her tailbone at the bottom. June tried to push herself up, but her bloody hand slipped out from beneath her. She used the other to stand and hobbled toward the front door.

She paused, breathing in a bit of the wood smoke and regaining some control of her body. The small bits of glass came out easily enough from her palm, but examining her foot, she knew she would need tweezers or else the risk of breaking the shard off inside her was too great.

When she turned the knob, the wind threw open the door, greeting her like an old friend. The papers swirled in the space before her, taunting her with their accessibility before floating just out of reach.

Stepping off the porch and into the mud, she went after whichever paper was nearest. She had to switch arms every few minutes, as the cut one would get too cold being stationary but go too numb from blood loss when not held against her.

This took most of the night.

The occasional flash of lightning from the distant hills would light her way, exposing a well-hidden page. The wind never took them far from the house, far from her, far from where they could be found, eventually. Once June could find nothing more among the rain and the wind and the cold, she trekked back inside, shivering and pale, her movement more like falling than taking steps, her pages clutched to her sopping robe.

The fire had gone well beyond the point of embers. She dropped her papers in front of the fireplace with a wet thud. She readied a fire but was shivering too thoroughly to strike a match. Peeling her robe and then her pajamas from her skin, the dried blood on her forearm, the mud caked among her pant legs and sleeves, the weight of the rain pushed the clothes into the deepest recesses of her body, until she could rely on nothing more than body heat. She took a deep breath, struck the match, and lit the fire.

Taking her pages with her, she sat on her chair in the firelight. Through the dirt and blood and grime, she tried to find any remaining words among the pages before falling asleep.

FINGERS

She told her husband her fingers were growing. "Not all at once, mind you. And they've always gone back."

He looked at her a moment, maybe waiting for the punchline, before removing the cat from his lap and holding out his own hand, inviting her to show him. Hesitating, she presented her left hand, just out of his reach. He pulled her the rest of the way in. From her thumb to her ring finger nothing seemed different, but her pinkie finger hung low, drooping, like each joint had detached from its partner. Her husband pinched it, wiggling it a bit. "Does this hurt?"

"No, it feels fine. I can even move it okay. See?" She tried to pull her finger from his grip, but it remained, stretching to fill the empty space and sagging between them from the weight.

They both stared at it for a moment before her husband broke the silence. "Hmmm. No, that's probably not good." He kissed the elongated finger on the nail and let it go. It fell to the floor with surprising speed. "Well, we'll see what it does tonight and get you to the doctor tomorrow, yeah?"

She looked for a moment at it, then at her husband, before hesitantly nodding to herself. "Yeah. Yeah, that's fine." She slumped off to the bedroom, her finger dragging along behind her, picking it up and holding it in her other hand only when the cat began to chase after and sunk in its claw.

The next morning the finger was back to normal.

"Guess there's nothing we can do then. Doctor can't diagnose something if there's nothing to see." He even gave it a little tug to confirm it would stay in place this time. "If it happens again, we'll take you to the emergency room, if you want. Since it's twenty-four hours."

She tugged on each of her fingers and sighed. They all stayed where they were. While her husband was at work, her fingers went in and out of place. As she vacuumed, her pinky almost got sucked up with the dirt before she realized. Her thumb was nearly taken out in the garbage disposal. The tip of her index finger was flayed as she diced scallions for dinner. But by the time her husband returned, aside from the bandage all her fingers were back in their place. When he asked about her day, she didn't mention them.

As the night went on, the problem came back. Chewing on the nail of her ring finger to relieve some of the nerves of the day, a particularly sharp tug unraveled it; it curled on the floor at her feet. When it reached its limit, she tried her best to put it back, but she already knew once it was out it would only go back of its own accord.

It took her husband a moment to notice, but once he did, he stared at it for a long time. She watched him, and she suspected he knew she was watching him, though his unmoving face did nothing to betray it. This lasted so long that when he finally broke the silence, she flinched. "So, is this just going to be a regular thing now?"

She didn't quite know what to say. Would it ever be normal? Is this the type of thing that can be normalized? Is this the type of thing that *should* be normalized? She could only muster an apology and try to collect her spiraling finger in her other hand to move to the bathroom so she could try to figure out how to fix it.

Halfway down the hall, the weight of her finger stretched all the fingers on her other hand to the ground. She looked up at her husband who was standing now, watching as she struggled to palm the mess of fingers that littered the floor. He approached her at a slow pace, as she held what she could to her chest with her arm and tried to make it the rest of the way to her destination. He was able to bridge the gap though and collected what remained on the floor in his hands. He traced one of the fingers up to her hand and rubbed it with affection, looked her in the eyes and said, "Okay, here I am. You have my attention. What's this really about?" Her fingers all did something they hadn't done before. They moved on their own, recoiling away from her husband, forming tangled webs behind her. Then all at once they returned to her hand as they should have been, as they were when she was born, when she first held hands, when she touched and felt, and the two of them, husband and wife, stared at each other for a moment before there was a metallic clanking on the cold tile and she was engulfed by her appendages, cocooned in the soft heat of herself.

CHAIR

|| the chair came from a schoolhouse that had closed decades before and even then it had begun to rust || but these days years of weathering had made the metal unrecognizable || placed in the yard against the fence || away from the house || before he was even born || a place for his father to sit and think || a tradition intended to be passed down || even if by force || his father sending him to that chair for all manner of reasons without regard to the state of the world || without regard for climate or weather || when the child needed correcting || the chair was the place for correction || made of hard wood || splintered || its coating long faded in all places that weren't kept from the elements || the curve of the seat cracked in a way that started to give if you favored one side or the other || encouraging him to learn to misbehave on the beautiful days || keep secrets of his indiscretions until the rain stopped or the summer sun was setting || even though he tried more than once to destroy the chair || sometimes when he was sent there || sometimes on his own accord || anticipating what may come || each time || his father making him fix it || reinforce it || make stronger what he harmed || just out of grasp of a furthered destruction || but as he felt as it was his father's chair it was his father's job || especially || since he was barely tall enough to see over the mower or strong enough to push it forward over the rough terrain with invisible holes hiding even more invisible creatures || but his father assigned it to him each summer || to

keep the yard mown and what better punishment than a trudge through the weeds in his shorts and long socks || catching stickers as they burrowed through his leg hairs and into his skin || a sharp pinch with every step || the summer sun adding sweat || adding salt || adding irritation || his face burning and his eyes watering each time he rubbed his hands through them || more and more attaching to his calves || this the reason he wore jeans deep into the summer || but not today || not when he thought he had more time || but his father attached him to that seat earlier and earlier each year || school having only just ended || not even a path to use left by deer or foxes or coyotes || just weeds folding over each other || the ground still soft with the last bits of moisture || and he sits in that chair and cleans off his legs and tries to remember if any of the pain felt deeper or more pronounced than the rest and then wondering if it really matters whether he noticed it or not when it happened because what mattered then were the two puncture marks just above his ankle and the way they bled different and the way in the hot summer breeze the path he took to get there was already blowing upright and in the distance sat his father by the back door || having placed a chair from the kitchen || flicking his cigarette into his coffee before taking a sip ||

GOODWILL

There's little use in sentimentality.

At least that's what the banker tells me. His watch, he paid more for it than I'm behind on my mortgage, and he checks it while I ask him a question about eviction, but he corrects me. Tells me it's a foreclosure. He uses the phrase, squatters' rights. Tells me to talk to my lawyer, even though I already told him there's no public defender for this kind of thing. This conversation is boring him, I can tell. For me, it's life or death. For him, it's a missed tee-time.

So, I have to tell the family, if it doesn't fit in the van it doesn't go. Our second car, we had to sell it just to keep the house as long as we did, so we have forty-eight hours until we're trespassing on bank property, and it's my little girl who has the bright idea to pawn our stuff, except we'd never be able to afford it back. So maybe we donate it.

We're packing boxes full of toys and gifts and writing I Wish and Here's Hoping and we're dropping everything off at Goodwill on the dream that our things only have value to us. We see some of our nicer things, things we bought for last Christmas maybe, and it all still looks too new. So my little girl, she takes her dollhouse, the prize gift from that year, and she throws it down the stairs. She sits on it and bounces and bends the plastic as best she can. My wife, she's taking out single screws from our electronics, removing the springs from the battery terminals. My son opens all of our board games and takes out the main pieces, keeps them in his pockets. We go to work mangling our luxuries. Just enough.

It becomes a family game, figuring out how to trick them. We take our bedsheets, stain them yellow and brown and red with food coloring. All of our pots and pans, we run huge scratches through the non-stick coating. We crack the glass on our picture frames and keep our own photos in them. If it was painted, we scuffed it. If it was sewn, we tore it. If it meant something to us, we destroyed it.

FLOWERS

My mother called it fertilizer.

Really, it was just ash from her cigarettes.

My father, the florist, the botanist, the gardener, had pots all over the house. And where there weren't pots, there were old shoes, or suitcases. Cooking pans, hollowed-out books, anything that could support the base amount of soil necessary to grow something. Anything.

For my mother, it meant unlimited ashtrays.

These are the only two activities I ever learned growing up. Some fathers play catch with their kids. Some mothers teach their children how to read. I learned how to make oxygen. And how to destroy it.

When I was born, they feared I was allergic. To anything. All of it. Everything. Long bouts of sneezing and coughing started right after I came into the world. The combination of herbs and spices and houseplants, all swirling their pollen at each other, mixing and matching and combining with smoke was too much for my infant sinuses to handle.

In fact, the cigarettes are why my father started gardening in the first place. To cover the smell of smoke, he planted peace lilies and English ivy. When my mother started getting stomach pains, he grew ginger. When my mother started getting treatment, he grew guarana. He even grew tobacco for her when the doctors insisted she quit smoking but she refused.

When my mother finally died, my father wilted.

So, I took up my parent's two favorite pastimes. The garden started in the house, but not everything can grow indoors. I had spent enough time watching my father to know how to lay out everything, and soon there were rows of seeds surrounding the property. As they grew, though, I barely noticed them. Cigarette in one hand and watering can in the other, all I could see were the sections of the lot that were still empty. And so, row after row was added, pushing out toward the old wooden fence that marked the property line.

Each flower and herb and vegetable required different amounts of water, so I watered them each with a personal touch, dragging out watering cans and buckets and hoses to each according to their need. Most of my time was spent in the garden. I always had water with me, and I could wander through the foliage with ease and grab food from a vine or a tree or the ground, almost anywhere.

My favorites were the flowers though. I watched as the bees landed inside them, doing their invisible work. More and more, I planted flowers instead of vegetables, admiring the beauty of the yard.

When the garden reached the fence, I uprooted the vegetables to make room for more flowers.

When those came in short supply, I uprooted the house.

At first, I used planters, but there was not enough sunlight to reach all of my plants, so I removed the roof. When the space between planters was better utilized for housing my flowers, I tore up the carpet, chiseled away at the tile, dug up the foundation to expose the cool earth below. After I removed the walls, the house was ideal for living things.

I stood next to the pipe that had once protruded from the side of the house, the one that fed water into the hose, the only remaining evidence that a house had ever stood, smoking a cigarette and admiring my handiwork. I had dug up every rock, leveled all the land, planted seeds between seeds between seeds to make use of every available space.

I took a deep breath. The air smelled sweet, sickly, filtered through a hazy trail of smoke.

I had taken to lying among my flowers, soft as they were, hugging my body to sleep. There were small indents all around where I had tried to find the perfect bed. I had not yet dared the sharper plants, doubting their ability to provide comfort, but found some undisturbed tulips littered among patches of red roses and prickly pears, even some thorn-bearing shrubs, and closed my eyes to rest. When I awoke, the smell of smoke had overtaken the sugar in the air. My eyes followed my hand where a cigarette had been, to where a small fire had caught on a petal, to the blaze quickly overtaking everything.

Before seeing it, I knew the hose would be melted. My only source of water. As if noticing me, the fire began to make its way toward the unburned plant life behind me. I made for the fence, running along it, knowing that it would be the last time I ever saw any of those flowers.

Along the fence, I searched for something I knew wasn't there because I had never seen it before. I had hoped that keeping my eyes to the ground for so long while planting meant I just hadn't noticed a gate in the fence.

No such luck.

I stumbled over the wavy leaves of a calathea plant in order to get enough height to clamber over the fence. Losing my balance, I expected to fall on hard, unwelcoming, unplanted ground and braced myself for a few seconds, just long enough for me to realize it was too long.

Wind rushed past my ears as I opened my eyes. A softness overtook me, coupled with a light tingle. I had never felt so weightless. Before me was a wall of sheer rock, above which, smoke billowed into the sky. The bits of fence I could still see from the edge were consumed in flame. I looked as long as I could, until my eyes started to burn. I opened my mouth in response to the pain and it filled with water, but not like the water I was used to. It was bitter, like the taste of skin.

The wind pushed and pulled the fragrant smoke down to me. I instinctively felt for the cigarettes in my pocket, wet and soggy and useless. The salt dried my tears before they could come, but I felt like crying, knowing that just out of reach, above the cliffs I had descended, there was nothing I could do to preserve the life I had taken such care to create.

I felt like a failure, never wanting to plant again, never wanting to risk the destruction of what I had promised life, had helped to flourish, and then neglected in the worst way. There I remained, floating in the water, unable to soak in anymore, feeling dry and pruney, staring at the fire as if it were the sun, wanting to look on even as it hurt my eyes. As night came and the only light was from the glow of the embers, I pushed myself down, daring myself to go deeper, to hold my breath a second longer. It was empty, empty as anything had ever been empty.

Empty.

It was empty until it wasn't.

Until I found the bottom and the rows of seaweed and coral.

Until the water was so encompassing that I needed only to provide the seeds. And so, I dug.

APPRAISAL

The Appraiser sat by the window of The Crossroads Motel, another in the string of cheap lodgings Gerald utilized nightly. As soon as she spoke, she saw his body tense. Although he was facing away from her, The Appraiser could imagine just what was happening. She'd seen it countless times before: The way he tried to rationalize a voice at this hour of the morning by letting the red glow of the digital clock blind him until his eyes adjusted; the way he wondered if it had been the television he'd left on to help him sleep, though no seedy establishment like this would have TV speakers nice enough to resonate the way her voice did; the way he wondered if he'd actually heard his own name. Additionally, The Appraiser was on the opposite side of the room from the television, quite by design.

Then there was the way Gerald tested his mattress, to see if he could roll over without the springs giving him away. Calling himself a coward in his head, knowing it was ridiculous to assume anyone was in his room talking to him, but still refusing to roll over, finally gaining the courage to turn on the lamp, still not rolling over. Sometimes her boss complained that theatrics like this were part of the reason she was so far behind, but if she couldn't have fun on the job, what was the point?

What made all of this worthwhile was the squeal of shock every middle-aged man made when they finally had the guts to roll over. Gerald was no exception. From his vantage, as with those who came before him, Gerald saw the figure of a woman, in a suit that didn't just say professional, but said intentional, holding a clipboard bursting with papers.

From her chair, she saw Gerald, a man who opted for all personal relationships to be business relationships, and all business relationships to die with the onset of night. When he rolled over and jumped back, it took all she had in her not to smile. "Gerald Holloway." She paused. "Do you remember that night? Do you remember your offer?" This was another one of her little cruelties. Even among those she appraised who did remember, most could not recall with the immediacy she required, not when waking from a dead sleep to find a stranger in their room. Gerald was the exception in this case, though. He remembered much of what he had said on the night of his graduation, alcohol aside. High school held some of his most vivid memories, since it had been the last time he did anything memorable.

"Gerald, at just seventeen you offered to sell your soul to someone very powerful. In exchange for this soul, you wanted to play music for a living. More specifically," she flipped through the pages on her clipboard, though they could have been blank as all the information she needed was already in her head, "you wished to play rock music. You were sitting in the car with one William Perez drinking beer and testing his new speakers. I have a quote here if you'll indulge me, 'Billy, listen, man, I'd sell my soul to play guitar like him. Imagine the *tail* he pulls, man. Not that I'm doing too bad in that department, but going town to town like that. No strings, man. No strings.' And it just sort of keeps going on like that from there. Afterward you throw a beer bottle at a passing car, which you miss, but a bit later a man gets a flat tire from the glass and is late to the birth of his daughter. Gerald, do you understand what I'm doing here?"

He leaned against the headboard, taking in the figure before him, controlling his breathing to steady his heart rate; he recognized that if he were in danger, it was not within his power to prevent it. Besides, in his line of work he was used to hearing eccentric people tell long-winded stories, though they were more often about their own lives and not his. Taking his opportunity to speak, though unsure what to say, he opted for his go-to with high tension conversations. "My friends call me Jerry."

"Who?" The Appraiser flipped through the pages on the clipboard again. "Listen, Gerald," she continued. "Is it still for sale or not? There's a whole process to this and we're not getting any younger. I mean, only one of us is aging but you take my point." No one had ever laughed at that joke but to her it was almost better that way; she never gave up on telling it.

Gerald took stock of his belongings. His suitcase for clean clothes and his other suitcase for dirty laundry. His beat-up car parked outside, mocking him every time it took a couple tries to get started. His trunk of wares, a vague collection of artifacts, antiques, cure-alls, poisons, instruments, utensils, self-help books, the latest technology, tools, tonics, toys, weapons, and anything else he could convince the average person they always needed but didn't know they were missing before having met him. It was an honest living, even if it wasn't really honest and wasn't really a living.

"So, you're saying I can sell my soul and become a famous musician? Just like that?" Gerald's experience as a salesman had made him skeptical of anyone else trying to sell him anything, but especially something that seemed too good to be true.

"That's what I'm here to find out. But I need your permission to examine it before I can say for certain."

Gerald hesitated. "What do you need from me?"

Almost as soon as he asked, The Appraiser ripped out a paper from the clipboard and passed it to Gerald along with a pen. "This is your basic appraisal consent form. Gives me access to the contents of your soul without handing over ownership. Need you to initial here saying you alone have full ownership of the soul in question or have been given permission from the owning party to sell it; here saying you understand that having a soul appraised is not a guarantee that a deal will be made to the satisfaction of both parties; here saying you are not in possession of another's soul and that the one being appraised is your one true soul with which you were born; here to waive the appraisal fee as part of our new millennium special; and here to confirm your name is spelled correctly. Then just sign and date."

The Appraiser whistled and spun around in her chair as Gerald took the time to read each section in full, something most clients didn't bother to do, but once he had, he did as he was told. "Okay, excellent. Now lie back on the bed. This shouldn't hurt, but the first time is usually a bit overwhelming. It's better to not run the risk of you falling."

Gerald scooted out flat. "First time? Do I have more than one soul?"

"No, no, of course not. Sometimes people's souls just aren't what they should be, so they opt to raise their values before selling. Try to get a better deal. Of course, they usually die before they get a second appraisal, with the queue being what it is now. It's not like when Elvis saw Chuck Berry and a week later I was having him sign the same papers. Now we have The Appraiser strike, outsourcing duties to The Damned which, let me tell you, it takes so long to train them to do anything you might as well just have The Trainers become Appraisers. It's why it took thirty years to get to you. Anyway, I don't want to bore you with bureaucracy. Hold still."

The Appraiser held her palm flat over Gerald's chest. For a moment nothing happened but all at once The Appraiser withdrew her hand and held in it a ball of swirling light. Gerald felt weightless, like he could float away if he allowed it, light-headed but with a distinct and clear focus.

Gerald's soul felt cool in her hand. Through it she could see a lifetime of decisions, intentions, outcomes, doors held open for strangers, red lights ran, heartfelt compliments, unsolicited attention, all thoughts and actions laid bare before her in an instant.

"Gerald, I'll be honest with you, your soul wasn't worth much when you offered it at seventeen, but now there's almost nothing to go off of here. You'd have better luck becoming a rockstar if you let me run your credit score which," she turned the soul to the side and focused her eyes, "I didn't even realize could go below 300."

The soul grew brighter as more was revealed, drowning out the dim yellow of the bedside lamp. What felt cold to The Appraiser bathed Gerald in warmth. He was calmer than he had been all his life. She took one last long look into the soul before closing her fist around it, diminishing the light. As it returned to Gerald's body, he felt all its weight; his chest felt heavy with a familiar sorrow he had not known was there until it was gone.

"Listen, Gerald, let me be direct. You're not going to become some big celebrity. The value isn't there. There's no return on investment. But hey, we're always happy to work with clients. This isn't an all-or-nothing business."

Gerald was only half-listening. He was overtaken by the way he had felt moments before; that freedom.

"Do you know what a cover band is, Gerald? I think if I made a couple calls, I could convince them to let you get good enough to play a bar somewhere. On Friday nights, even. You'd just have to find a nice place to settle down. Not a lot of touring for cover bands. Though The Fab Four have made a few million at this point. It says in the handbook not to play genie but sometimes I can't help it. 'I'd sell my soul to play like The Beatles,' like, c'mon, you're asking for that to be misinterpreted."

Gerald turned to look The Appraiser in the eye. "How do you take my soul? Is it the same as just now?"

The Appraiser smiled. "The very same. Only when I close my hand it's gone forever, even out of my own reach."

"So I would just feel . . ." he trailed off. He tried to return to even a modicum of that weightlessness.

"Yes." The Appraiser realized what he was asking. Though frowned upon, this was a recognized and valid reason to accept a soul. There was a reputation to uphold, and, even if consensual, word getting out that they were taking souls in exchange for nothing would damage the brand. "Or not feel." She tore another paper from the clipboard and held it to him, this time with no pen. "Just press your thumb against the paper." Toward the bottom of the page was a slight indent, a needle, which would draw just enough blood to bond the sale.

The Appraiser watched Gerald's chest rise and fall as he measured the pressure of each breath. Her eyes moved to his face as he turned to match her gaze. He smiled, a smile she returned, before their faces fell flat. For the first time since she arrived, both of them noticed the soft voices of the television as it cut to commercial.

TEETH

When the first tooth breaks, I think little of it. Teeth do break, after all. So I go to the dentist, who refers me to an orthodontist, who refers me to a cosmetic dentist, who charges me more than the first two combined to install a veneer. A fake incisor that stands out worse than when it was broken, all clean and white and porcelain. He tells me to stay away from hard foods and I should be fine. That the rest of my teeth look strong. Floss and brush twice a day, he tells me. Okay, I lie.

The thing I don't tell him, tell any of them, is that my jaw hurts from grinding my teeth at night. Not even when I'm asleep. I just sit there, staring at the TV or maybe out the window and work my jawbone. It makes my ears ring all day and sometimes the next time I eat, it's like chewing a handful of sand. But with my new tooth, I tell myself maybe I'll try to stop.

It works for a little bit until I stop paying attention and catch myself doing it again, and who knows how long I've been doing it, except my fillings feel hot so probably a little while, so I bite down as hard as I can, preventing any movement, only that hurts worse. The sides of my tongue are rubbed raw and sometimes I think I can taste blood except the last few years I feel like I can barely taste anything at all, so I just hold my mouth open.

My jaw still moves through the air and my tongue starts to hurt more with the exposure. There's salt in the kitchen, big rock salt, so I pour some in because I can't tell if blood is starting to pool in my mouth or if it's just extra spit but I'm too afraid to check, like I don't trust my own jaw not to bite off my finger in revenge, but the rock salt is sharp and now my eyes are watering and my mouth is too dry, like the kind of dry you feel when you suck your teeth, that cold air dry where all you want to do is close your mouth, so I do and I bite down on all that salt and it shatters and scrapes across everything. And I'm drinking water, first from a glass and then straight from the tap, and I'm swishing it around and adding more salt and crunching it and my tongue is burning and I think I'm outright crying now.

My gums feel like they're bleeding too and my mouth is dry from the salt but I keep pouring water in to make up for it until my stomach starts to hurt, but at this point I'm not sure if there's even salt left or if I broke another tooth, or maybe all my teeth, except I know my new one still stands tall and proud because my tongue shoots out to check its condition and for a brief and glorious moment, I feel safe before biting clean through.

EULOGY

When James asked for the time off, he was certain his boss thought he was lying. He tripped over the words, even though he had practiced them, even though there were only three he needed to say to convey the whole message, the whole message and much more. All the same, he couldn't say them at first.

Looking in the mirror of his hotel room, his puffy eyes lit up at the idea of his boss sitting in his office scouring the obituaries over his morning coffee, looking for a woman who shared James' last name, taking the lack of evidence as proof of deceit.

It's not that James didn't like his boss. He did, as much as one could like a boss. He just felt an odd sort of shame about asking for the time. "A lot of mothers dying this month," was all his boss had said before walking away, but moments later James received an email confirming his time off request had been approved. Three days bereavement leave, unpaid. He would have to go to HR to get reimbursed once he had proof of death in hand.

James didn't know how to tie a tie, no matter how much he tried, no matter how many different ones he went through. Jenny always tied them for him. He used to joke that he took the house, but she took his RSVP's to formal events. Was it better to show up in a crooked tie, knot fat and loose at the top, resting halfway up his gut or in no tie at all?

It was decided. No tie. Who would say anything to him today anyway? He could go in his pajamas if that's how he chose to grieve. Who tied his tie at his father's funeral? He could only picture the figure of a woman with Jenny's face, bending down to straighten his suit, kissing him on the forehead, but that couldn't have been. He was just a boy when his father died. He had lost his father before he lost his belief in Santa.

He rubbed his cheeks. The coarse resistance of the stubble soothed him for a moment but then it struck him. He had already emptied his bag of toiletries, showered, and brushed his teeth since checking in, but he did not remember seeing a razor. His half-hearted attempts at rummaging through his empty duffel bag brought no relief.

Okay. No tie. No shave. Might as well lose the jacket at this point. He rubbed his temples, his eyes, wiped his mouth, leaving his hand there an extra beat, enjoying the residual scent of his breakfast orange still emanating from his fingers.

Was there a point in even going? They would just want him to speak, to stand in front of God and all and talk about himself, talk about his mother. Maybe he'd try the underwear trick, dressing down everyone in his head. Was it an open casket?

From the nightstand his phone began to vibrate. He eyeballed its reflection in the mirror but made no move toward it, his gaze pausing briefly on the clothes strewn out on the bed before returning to his own face. It had been years since he had really looked in the mirror, took himself in, *reflected*, he laughed to himself. He imagined he'd looked like this for some time, all sagged and swollen, but he felt comfortable blaming it on the occasion. *Lack of sleep* even though he had gone to bed earlier the previous night than he had since Jenny. *Jet lag* even though it was only a three-hour drive from his house to his hotel room and they were in the same time zone. *Eyes puffy from sadness* even though he hadn't cried once since he heard the news.

The phone did its dance on the nightstand again. He knew it was Jenny. She had called seven times that morning. Never left a message. The last time he spoke to her was about a week before when she told him he needed to call one of his siblings, his brother or his sister, didn't matter which one because they couldn't get ahold of him. Before that they hadn't spoken in three years.

If he did decide to speak, what would he say? Who was going to go to this funeral anyway? Who would see him, all dressed up but still dressed down, no one fully making eye contact, breaking away from hugs and handshakes before they're asked to sit and stand and roll over? His siblings, sure. They're who made him come out in the first place, and they'd act extra sad in all the ways he couldn't.

He needed a jacket.

No, a jacket was too far. He tried to picture himself up there, all eyes on him, passing off awkward jokes as heartfelt memories. In his head he was wearing a jacket, but he couldn't trust his head. In his head his tie was tied perfectly too. Maybe he'd talk about how he can't tie a tie. Could his mom tie a tie?

Another buzz from his phone, this time coupled with a knock.

No one knew where he was staying, but in a small town like this there were only so many options.

Jenny was calling again. And knocking. She'd make him wear a tie. And shave. He slapped his cheeks, rubbed his eyes, wiped his face. He couldn't smell the orange anymore, just the cologne he was wearing. Jenny hated that cologne.

He knew what she would say to him, looking the way he did, dressed the way he was. That morning he had wanted to go in his sweatpants. As far as he was concerned, the fact that he was in slacks was progress, even if she wouldn't see it that way.

The phone stopped and immediately started again as the knocking grew louder. He walked toward the door, then changed paths and answered his phone instead. The lamp next to the bed was the only light in the room and moving this close to it made his eyes ache.

Hello? . . . I'm out getting breakfast . . . I'm not too sure. I just found a place . . . I know I grew up here, but that doesn't mean I have every restaurant memorized . . . Okay, well I won't be back for a while . . . No, don't wait there, you should have some breakfast too . . . Shit, is it really? Well, lunch then . . . Uh, no, I don't know how to get here, I just walked until I found a place. I'm sure I'll find my

way back . . . I'll ask the server when they bring me my check . . .
Yeah, I could just ask what the restaurant is called but . . . Hang
on.

The deadbolt felt heavy in his hands as he removed the only
thing standing between him and the outside world. The cold
noon air bit at his face as he squinted through the sunlight
drenching his face through the open door. A jacket was a must
now. He didn't want to spend the entire funeral shivering.

Jenny looked him in the eye, gave him a quick up and down, then
focused all her attention inside the motel room and walked past
him. She slid open the curtains, light revealing the dust of the
room as it settled on everything in sight. "Come here," she stated
flatly.

He approached her, shuffling his feet, unable to make eye
contact. When he was within a couple feet of her, he opened his
arms a bit, anticipating a hug, but she swiftly grabbed his elbows
and returned them to his side, taking a step back as she instead
began fiddling with his shirt buttons. "I'm not sure this is the
right time, Jen."

"Don't be an idiot. Can't you go one day without making some
dumb joke? It's your mother's funeral, for Chrissake. No wonder
Will doesn't want you there."

"Sorry," he mumbled. He looked down to realize he had missed
a button when he put on his shirt. "Wait, Will doesn't want me
there?"

"When's the last time Will wanted you anywhere? *Hold. Still.* It's not that he doesn't want you there. It's just that he's afraid of what you'll do." He stared at her mouth when she talked, but thinking she couldn't look at him while she was fixing his shirt dared a glance at her eyes. She noticed immediately, locking eyes with him and he opted to stare over her head at the dated wallpaper behind her. She buttoned his top button. He rubbed his throat at the added pressure.

She moved to the mess on the bed and began folding his clothes, smelling them as she went to determine if they were clean or dirty. As she stared down at one shirt in particular, hoping it might tell her if it was freshly worn or just poorly washed, James moved back to the mirror opposite. He hoped his lopsided shirt was the reason he kept ending up with a lopsided tie, even though he knew it wasn't. "Speaking of people who shouldn't be places, what are you doing here?"

"I was asked to come . . ."

" . . . The fox chases the bunny around the tree. No . . ."

" . . . You know I stayed close with your mother after . . ."

" . . . Around and around and around the tree. Shit . . ."

" . . . And Liz's separation is going about as well as you'd expect . . ."

" . . . The bunny got away . . ."

" . . . So she came to me since I have experience divorcing petulant manchildren . . ."

" . . . Ah, yes, I remember your first husband well."

"Child*ren*. Plural." James looked at Jen in the mirror and made a snarky face. She turned to him as if she hadn't seen it. "Did you finally learn how to tie a tie?"

"You tell me." He spun around, enthusiastically framing the tie with his hands.

"Okay, I guess I'll do that for you too." With one forceful tug she loosened the tie completely, measuring it on either side and began the intricate dance of folds that made a Windsor Knot. "Wait, you haven't shaved. Why is your shirt on if you still have to shave? White shirts and black stubble do not mix."

"I didn't bring a razor."

"I'm surprised you managed to bring yourself." She cleared her throat. "You seriously didn't bring a razor?"

"I thought I did, but apparently not." Before he could register it happening, Jen produced a razor from James' duffle bag. She wrapped it in a dark blue shirt she had folded earlier and tossed it at him.

"Put on this shirt over your shirt. Shave. Take it off again. Do your best not to make an absolute mess of your clothes, please."

James stared at her for a moment until he remembered. She always made him put important items in a side pocket so he could easily check that they were there before he left and easily find them when he needed them. Except he always remembered to fill that pocket when packing but never to empty it when he arrived.

"I can't shave you. I can't hold a razor that close to your throat. Not when people know I'm with you."

This snapped him out of his confusion. He sauntered away and flinched at the state of his face under the harsh fluorescents of the bathroom. Here the shadows under his eyes shrouded the color of his face, except his cheeks and nose, which shone red with tiny veins. He hesitated for a moment, afraid of the condition the rest of his face might be in beneath the thin layer of hair obscuring it, but he knew he wouldn't be allowed out of the bathroom until he did as he was told, so he slid on the extra shirt. It was tight across his dress shirt and made it hard for him to lift his arms. He turned on the water, wet his face, and worked at the hairs.

As he shaved, Jen came in and out of the bathroom, grabbing his travel shampoo and body wash. "Were you a big enough boy to use this this morning?" she asked, waving his toothbrush in front of him.

He nodded as much as he could without removing the razor from his face. "Good." She went back into the bedroom and James could hear the zipper and rattle of his duffel bag as it was worked back and forth. When he was clean shaven, he joined her. "Give me that shirt now." He struggled a bit but managed to pull it over his head, inside out, and tossed it to her. She put it right side out, shoved it in his bag, and zipped it closed. "Is that all we need? Are you good? Your jacket's here," she tossed it to him, "and your shoes are by the bed."

He looked at his jacket in his hands for a beat and slumped over. "I can't go."

"The fuck you can't. Even if Will's being, shall we say, extra cautious, that doesn't mean you can leave Liz alone. You know he won't do anything for her."

"I can't go because what am I going to say?"

"Say? What d'you mean 'say'?"

"The eulogy. I have to speak. If I go, I have to speak, and I can't speak, so I can't go." He made for the bed and sat, slouching into his hands.

Jen walked over but did not join him, instead towering over him, making him feel her gravity. "You don't have to speak. Shit, no one really wants you to speak. You can barely tell a good story at a party among friends. Why would we expect you to tell a touching story about your mom?"

"Isn't that worse?" He sat up, looked at her, looked past her at the water-stained ceiling. "*Why isn't James speaking? Oh, it's because he's such an embarrassment to the family. Oh, it's because he has nothing good to say. Oh, it's because he can't process grief in a way we are comfortable with so we keep him locked away."*

"Oh, come on, it's not like that and you know it. Everyone wants to hear you speak. They just don't want you to tell another story about how you don't know how to tie a tie. Could have just learned how in all the time you've spent telling those stories. No, we want to hear you talk about your mom and what she meant to you. We want to hear you talk about this family like it's your family. Liz wants it. Will wants it. I want it." She took a deep breath. James knew that was a sign that she was getting angry and trying to calm down, one of the tricks their therapist had taught them. "Shit, I married into this goddamn family and I still have more to say about being a part of it than you do. Put on a fucking smile, and then a fucking frown, and then a fucking smile again, and act like the son of a dead mother."

There was a heavy silence.

James collapsed back on the bed.

Jen paced the floor for a second, went into the bathroom, double-checked that she got all his belongings, trying to find something to distract her.

James reached for the nightstand, grabbed the remote, and turned on the television. She turned it off from the set.

He turned it on again.

Jen unplugged it from the wall, grabbed the remote from his hand, and threw it back at him, missing his face by an inch.

He sat up again, let his anger well inside him, smacked the bed with open palms, let out a grunt, and slipped on his shoes, tying them slowly.

Jen continued to pace until he stopped moving and cleared his throat in a way that let her know it was time.

"Okay, let's go," said James, defeated by the weight of his own guilt. Of course he would go to his mother's funeral. And he would shake his big brother's hand and give his little sister a hug and maybe even look his ex-wife in the eye and smile and neither of them would look away out of shame. "Jen?"

"No, this is on you. I have done all I can. I got you dressed. I packed your clothes. I made you shave. You have literally nothing else you have to do besides get there. So, get there." She opened the door and stared at him; to him she was nothing more than a blinding silhouette. "I'm not your mother, James. She's dead." A look crossed her face that James had not seen in a long time. It was the pain she wore when she realized she had hurt someone else. It was better than any apology James had ever received: unfiltered remorse. "Get there."

He made it as far as the door, watching her walk across the motel balcony past the other rooms, each indistinguishable from the next, watching her descend the cement staircase in hard echoes as the thin metal sheets supporting each step vibrated, watching her get in her car and stare at him for just a moment, just long enough for him to give a soft smile, watching her reverse and drive out of the parking lot, turning right behind the surrounding buildings. He patted his pockets, checked for his keys, his wallet, his phone. It was all there. All he would need for the night.

But instead of closing the door behind him, he went back inside the room, loosened his tie, and cried.

STARS

I had never been to the ocean before.

I grabbed fistfuls of the sand surrounding me and held them above my body, imagining all the galaxies they could contain. The grains freed themselves from my fingers and tumbled onto my stomach. The pile grew, covering half my torso. I was blinded in every direction by the sun reflecting across the morning clouds, and the glare forced its way through my closed eyes, leaving a red tinge. Chills ran through my body from the damp earth and dawn breeze. I put on the jacket I had been using as a pillow and let the sand fall through my legs. The salt in the air burned my nose the way the chlorine had done the first time I had ever swum.

***

Hypnotized, I stared into the soft water, standing in line next to four other girls, all wearing the same one-piece bathing suit. A rope dotted with blue and white floats that glared with fresh plastic ran the width of the pool to separate the safety of the shallow end from the freedom of the deep. The first thing the instructor told us was never to go past the rope. She explained that one day we would be allowed on the other side, but for now we should imagine an invisible wall that only permitted certified swimmers past it. I begrudgingly watched those swimmers maneuver through their side with grace and certainty. Some

63

made it from one end of the pool to the other with little effort; others dove and contorted their bodies in peculiar ways, but they always hit the water with the tips of their fingers, enveloped almost instantly. I knew where I wanted to be.

The instructor let us choose the lanes where we would learn to swim. The other girls clamored and shoved to get the one closest to the restrictive safety of the wall running along the shallowest part of the pool. I stepped to the lane nearest the rope and stood over it with pride, prepared to conquer the small waves that lapped against the concrete border. She paced behind us, stating that on her whistle, we should sit on the edge of the pool, put in our feet, and as we got comfortable, lower ourselves in, never letting go of the edge. The wall was our friend. It would keep us safe.

The other girls weren't all brave at once. The first sat far from the pool and scooted toward the water. The others followed suit. While they gathered their courage, I plopped right down on the edge, letting the water swallow my feet. The gentle tickle from my new friend made me giggle. I held onto the edge and slid in, almost losing my grip on the wall but supporting my weight with the tips of my fingers. It was overwhelming how light I felt, floating. I spat out the water that entered my mouth through a smile I could not control. This was a freedom I never wanted to lose.

Six weeks later, there we stood again, ready to be certified. We waited, our backs to our lanes. This was the first time I had seen any of the other girls in their street clothes. It was strange being so near the water in jeans and tennis shoes. The instructor walked down the line, handing us certificates that were mostly blank aside from a border that resembled waves. All that mattered to me was my name across the top.

I didn't thank her with words, just an excitable squeal as I ran to my parents, placing the sheet in front of them like it was the most delicate object I'd ever held. Then, running at full speed, I jumped into the water, landing just in front of the rope. The voices of my parents and instructor carried across the water, shouts I mistook as encouragement. I looked at the deep end, then at my instructor, and smiled to express my gratitude for getting me here. She tentatively kicked off her shoes, gesturing and watching to see if I was going to come back to the wall.

Still grasping it in my fingers, I dunked my head and swung to the other side of the rope. There was nothing to stop me from exploring these waters. My heart pounded as I looked at the emptiness before me. I glanced at my instructor once more, who had since removed her shirt and was taking off her shorts, revealing the lifeguard-mandated swimwear underneath. I took a deep breath and let go.

I paddled with a new energy. The pressure in my nose and ears grew as my limbs flailed. The chlorine burned my eyes. I closed them.

My lungs ached. I had never been underwater this long before. I had never even held my breath like this before. How long could

I go? I remembered seeing a man on TV hold his breath for over ten minutes and wondered if that was normal.

A sharp, sudden pain radiated from the crown of my head. Was this normal too? First it hurts your eyes and ears, then your chest, then your head? Was the invisible wall fighting me, convinced I didn't belong over here, pulling me back? I tried to scream, but it was stolen by a series of bubbles that moved up before disappearing altogether. The pressure left my chest and transferred to my head. I couldn't breathe in again. This was all wrong. This wasn't swimming. Everything around me was blue and I couldn't move forward.

The instructor grabbed my arms and pulled me through the newly-explored waters. I took a deep breath as soon as the sun hit my face.

I had swum. I had swum the way I had been taught. It had almost killed me. I never forgave the wall for stopping my advance, but I craved the freedom it contained.

***

The clouds had cleared and the sun was almost directly above me. I draped my arm over my eyes to keep out the light. That morning I had lain in the middle of the dark sand where the water had been at high tide the night before, the shadow of the ocean's past lining my body. The warmth of the day had left it dry. I had traveled many years and miles to see the ocean but wanted it to come the rest of the way to meet me. Now it lapped at my feet, wetting them before sliding the sand out from under my heels. This was the first time I had ever felt the ocean. It was colder than I expected.

I spent my life looking forward to this first time. People often do. They spend their lives looking toward a first date, a first kiss, a first love, a first day.

What people never dwell on are lasts. Finales are a necessary consequence of premieres. Some firsts are a series of onlys; others become a series of agains. Some firsts are also lasts and it's these lasts that are never recognized as such.

They just are.

***

The night I graduated from high school, most of my classmates went to parties. Some went home. I went to the pool. It had been an exceptionally warm June and even late into the evening the water was still comfortable. There were no lights and the water was the kind of pure black that reflected the stars in a way that consumed them, like it needed to consume their light to survive.

I stepped into the pool from the shallow end, and as the water stopped at my waist, I was amazed at the thought of ever being at risk in these waters. There was more resistance with each step forward as the slant of the pool deepened. When I reached the fraying rope, my head was still above water, but only just. I tucked it under my chin, feeling the rough threads rubbing at my throat. The faded plastic floats bobbed lazily with the ripples my body made.

My fingers traced a circle on the center of my scalp. Even though the skin hadn't broken, I always swore there was a scar. I slid under the rope. My throat itched and I rubbed water on it to soothe the fresh irritation before swimming to the deep end and holding onto the wall, relaxing. I took a deep breath and pushed down. The dark pool happily consumed me too, reflecting nothing back to the surface.

***

The tide reached my calves, occasionally wetting as far up as my waist. Even though I knew to expect it, the cold still sent a shock through my body with every new inch it discovered. I noticed voices for the first time. Groups of people were spread out across the beach. Were any of them locals who dreamed of owning swimming pools? Perhaps a life of freedom had instilled in them a craving for walls.

Two children were laughing as they followed the tide into the ocean, trying to outrun it as the waves came back. Farther up the beach a couple was tearing pieces of bread and tossing them to a colony of seagulls. The birds shuffled back and forth, following the bait as the couple laughed. The children became bored with the tide and set their sights on the seagulls, running through them. They scattered temporarily before forgetting the danger and shuffling back in search of more.

The water climbed my back, wetting my shoulder blades before finally overtaking me. The weightlessness sent tension through my body, like missing a step when descending stairs. I was lifted by the water, pushed up the beach, pulled back down. Each time the water tried to take me with it but retreated faster than it could carry me, dropping me again in the sand; a million galaxies supporting my weight. With each cycle, the water stayed with me more, until I was floating inches above the sand, rocking back and forth with the crashing waves.

It carried me until I was parallel with the shore. I spread my arms and nudged away with the tips of my fingers, placing my feet in the shallows and pointing my head toward the horizon. The sand that had supported me throughout the morning scraped against my toes as I gave a final push into freedom.

The waves gave little resistance as I paddled with ease, rolling over their curves. It was refreshing, not coming to an end and having to turn around, but instead, understanding the surrounding endlessness. I had spent a lifetime swimming on calm waters, waters that only rose when escaping the weight of others.

There was no rope here to separate the shallow from the deep. There was only one wall, and I was swimming away from it. The clouds were starting to come in again, wrestling with the sun, casting short-lived shadows across my face. I continued to kick, arms outstretched like I was reaching for either end of the universe.

To make us feel small, astronomers tell us there are more stars in the universe than grains of sand on the beach. Did those scientists count all the grains of sand beneath the water? Could the same be said for each grain of salt the oceans contained? Floating through patches of seaweed, the nebulas teased my legs, offering support and tempting me to join them.

I treaded water and looked to the shore. There were the formless shadows of people on the beach. The wind had a chill again. The clouds were sparse now as the sun approached the horizon. I swam toward it.

I chased the sun I would never reach as it buffeted my head with violent oranges and reds. Every stroke brought me closer to my impossible destination until the ocean swallowed the day completely.

For a moment I treaded water again. I could no longer see the shore save for a few streetlights and a distant bonfire, eyes that would not blink. I shifted my weight so I was on my back again. The ocean was calm and reflected the sky, a massive darkness with small specks of light floating indifferently within. My ears were surrounded by water, leaving me with only the vibrations of my pounding heart, secrets whispered by the stars.

A shiver covered my body. I slipped my shoes from my feet. Then my socks. My jeans. Jacket, shirt, underwear. They descended into the black water. It felt warmer being exposed, even with my skin taut against the cold.

I watched the stars as they floated across the sky, a mirror that reflected nothing but time. I thought about the wall and fingered the crown of my head. My chest tightened. I felt like I was holding my breath even above water.

I inhaled as deeply as I could. The salty air coated my insides. The eyes that watched from the beach had all blinked. My heart pounded in my ears.

I exhaled, depressing my lungs. The water washed over my face. All I could taste was salt. It painted my lips and teeth as I smiled, the smile of a first time. The weight of the ocean extinguished the stars. I closed my eyes and sank into myself.

NOTES ON PREVIOUS PUBLICATIONS

Previous versions of these stories were published by Dollar Store Magazine, Fiery Scribe Review, Gastropoda Lit Mag, Haunted MTL, Querencia Press, Sledgehammer Lit, The San Joaquin Review, Warning Lines Magazine, and Wild Blue Zine.